THIS BOOK BELONGS TO

~~Marjorie~~   ~~Jerry Lee~~

....

....

LADYBIRD BOOKS

UK | USA | Canada | Ireland | Australia | India | New Zealand | South Africa

Ladybird Books is part of the Penguin Random House group of companies
whose addresses can be found at global.penguinrandomhouse.com.

www.penguin.co.uk   www.puffin.co.uk   www.ladybird.co.uk

Penguin
Random House
UK

Published in Australia by Puffin Books, 2022

This edition published in Great Britain by Ladybird Books Ltd, 2023
002

Text and illustrations copyright © Ludo Studio Pty Ltd 2022

Printed in China

The authorized representative in the EEA is Penguin Random House Ireland,
Morrison Chambers, 32 Nassau Street, Dublin D02 YH68

A CIP catalogue record for this book is available from the British Library

ISBN: 978-0-241-55059-5

All correspondence to:
Ladybird Books, Penguin Random House Children's
One Embassy Gardens, 8 Viaduct Gardens, London SW11 7BW

MIX
Paper from
responsible sources
FSC® C018179

BLUEY

EASTER

It's the night before Easter
at the Heeler house.

"Big sleep tonight, kids," says Dad.
"The **Easter bunny's** coming!"
"How do we know he won't forget us again?" Bingo asks.
"Yeah, like he did last year," adds Bluey.

"We've been through this. He didn't forget you," says Mum.
"Yeah, he was just late," agrees Dad.
"We **promise** he won't forget this time," says Mum.

"Do you think the Easter bunny will remember us?"

"Yeah, I do. Night, Bingo!"

But Bingo isn't so sure.

"Bingo, wake up!" shouts Bluey the next morning.

Bluey and Bingo check their Easter pouches.
There are **no chocolate eggs** inside.

"But wait," says Bluey.
"There's a box!"

"And a letter,"
adds Bingo.

"I think these are clues to where the Easter bunny has hidden our eggs," says Bluey. "Hmm. Letter . . . Box . . . Letter box!"

Bingo and Bluey run out to the letter box. Inside, there's a chatterbox.

Bluey sounds out, "EAST-ER EGG."

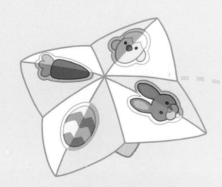

"What's your favourite colour?" she asks Bingo. "Blue – like you," says Bingo.

"It's a cook's hat, with an egg!" says Bluey.

"What does it mean?" asks Bingo.
"Cooks work in the kitchen . . . Maybe the Easter eggs are in the kitchen," says Bluey as they race off.

"I think the clue might be in the fridge," says Bluey.

"Bingo, look at the eggs!" says Bluey.
"The Easter bunny doesn't bring **normal** eggs," says Bingo.
"He brings **chocolate** eggs."
"I know, but look at the end one!" shouts Bluey.

"Dad, is there chocolate in this?" the girls ask. Dad chops the kiwi in half. "No chocolate," he says.

Bingo is disappointed. But, suddenly, Bluey understands the clue. "I think I know where the eggs are!"

Bingo and Bluey run to the playroom and look under the kiwi rug. **Still no eggs!**

"Maybe the Easter bunny likes other children more than me," says Bingo sadly. "No, Bingo, he likes you," Bluey says encouragingly.

Bingo spots an arrow on the rug. "It's pointing to the backyard," she says. "Come on, Bluey!"

They split up and search outside.

I DON'T REMEMBER THAT SANDCASTLE.

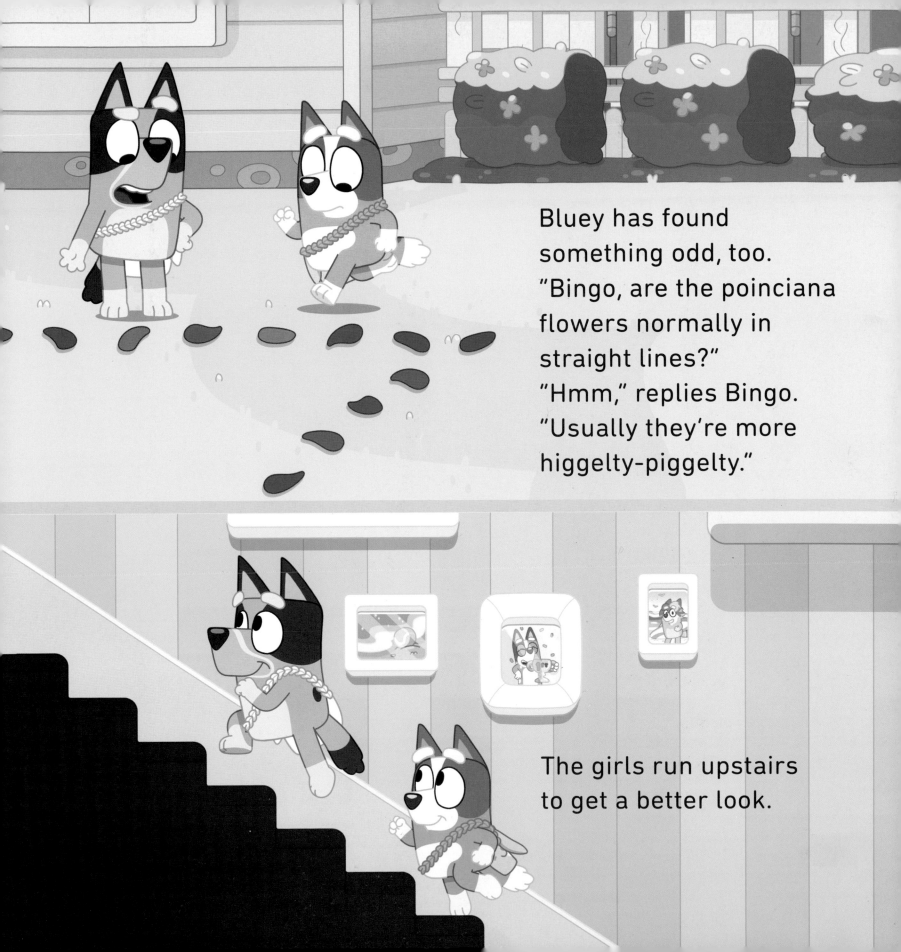

Bluey has found something odd, too. "Bingo, are the poinciana flowers normally in straight lines?" "Hmm," replies Bingo. "Usually they're more higgelty-piggelty."

The girls run upstairs to get a better look.

"It's a castle!" says Bluey. "Wait –
there's a castle in London.
We've got to get to the airport!"
Bluey races off.
"Wait, Bluey," says Bingo,
and Bluey stops. "I think it's
a **different** castle."

I HIT
SOMETHING!

IS IT
CHOCOLATE?

IT IS! IT IS!
WAIT . . . IT ISN'T.

"It's . . . toilet paper," says Bluey. Then she smiles. "Hang on, look –
eggs! It's another clue. Come on!"

Toilet paper belongs in the toilet, so Bluey and Bingo search the upstairs bathroom.

They search and search, but there's no chocolate.
Where else is there toilet paper?

OH NO! DAD'S TOILET!

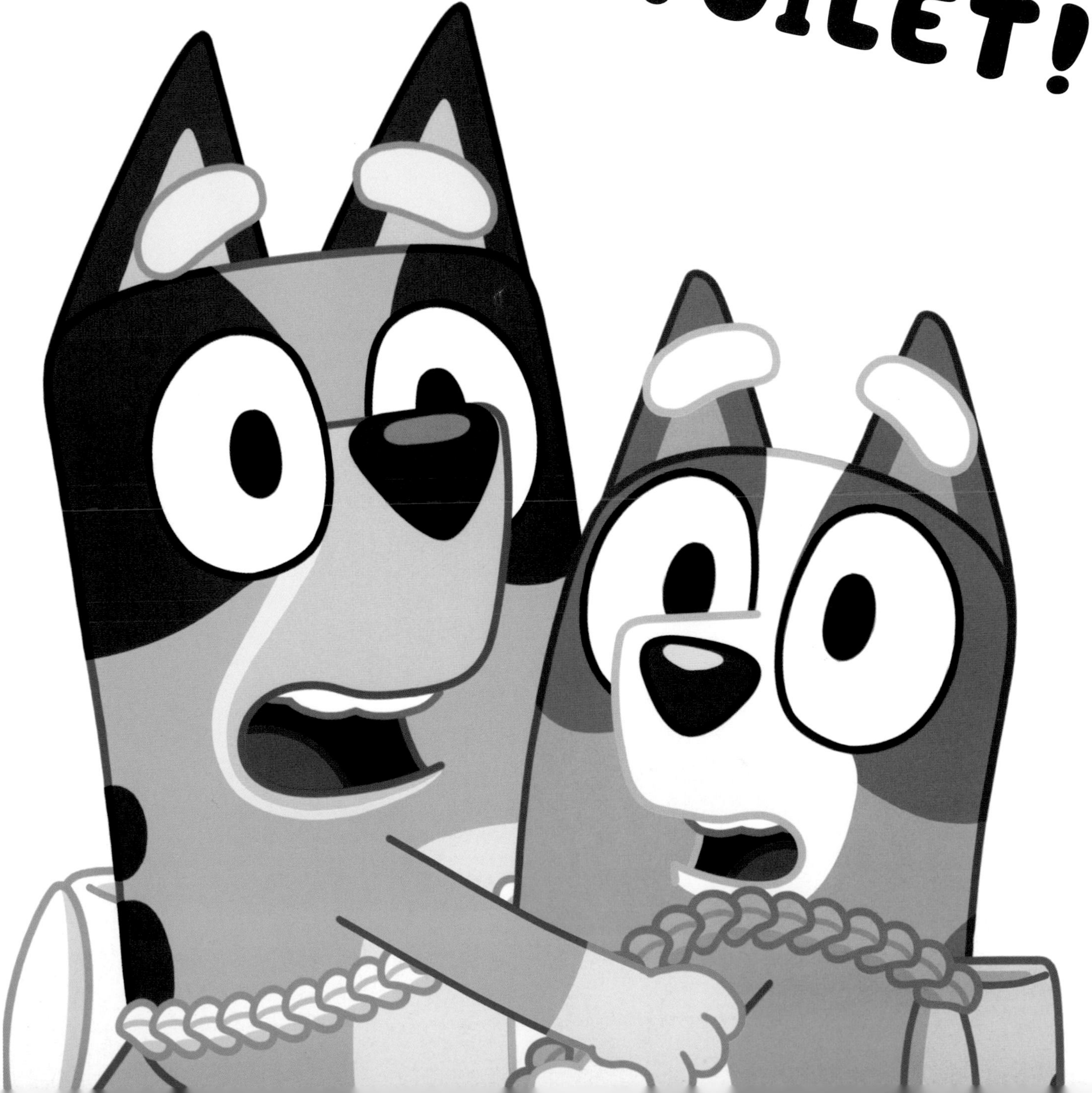

It stinks!

"Someone has to go in there," says Bluey.
"But it stinks so much we'll die!" Bingo complains. Then she says sadly, "Aw. There will be no Easter."
"Yes, there will be, Bingo," Bluey declares.

"I'm going in!"

Bluey tries to search for clues, but it's too stinky.
She collapses – and then she sees something familiar.

Bluey gives a sketch of the clue to Bingo.
"It's our **window!**" Bingo says.

"But we've already searched our room,"
Bluey replies.
"I knew it," sniffs Bingo. "The Easter bunny
has forgotten us. It's my fault. I'm just a
small, forgettable child."

"No, you're not, Bingo," Bluey says firmly. "You're a **great** child. You're smart. You figured out the castle clue all by yourself." Bingo smiles. "Yeah, I did."

"It's me who's forgettable," says Bluey.
"You are not!" Bingo replies. "You're brave – you went into Dad's stinky toilet!"
Bluey smiles now, too. "Yeah, I did. We're not forgettable!"
"Yeah, we're rememberable!" says Bingo.

Suddenly, Bluey spots footprints.
BUNNY FOOTPRINTS.
EASTER BUNNY
FOOTPRINTS!

The girls follow them. Out of the door . . .

down the hall . . . all the way to . . .

. . . Dad's study!

They roll away the yoga ball, until finally they find . . .

"He remembered us."